For my father
who always encouraged me to fly.

The Magic Sceptre™
The Legend of Blue Santa Claus
Text and Illustrations
Copyright © 2006 Joan K. Creamer
Printed in China

For information address
Silver Snowflake Publishing.
P.O. Box 1256, East Greenwich, RI 02818
www.TheMagicSceptre.com
First Edition
1 3 5 7 9 10 8 6 4 2
SAN: 8 5 0 – 3 9 4 X

Publisher's Cataloging-in-Publication
(Provided by Quality Books, Inc.)

Creamer, Joan Klatil.
   The magic sceptre : the legend of blue Santa Claus /
by Joan Klatil Creamer. -- 1st ed.
   p. cm.
   SUMMARY: Explains the special magic that allows Santa
to know what toys each child wants, visit all the
children in the world in one night without being seen,
and deliver gifts to houses with no chimneys.
   Audience: Ages 3-7.
   LCCN 2006902934
   ISBN-13: 978-0-9778476-3-1
   ISBN-10: 0-9778476-3-2

   1. Santa Claus--Juvenile fiction. 2. Christmas--
Juvenile fiction. 3. Magic--Juvenile fiction. [1. Santa
Claus--Fiction. 2. Christmas--Fiction. 3. Magic--
Fiction.]   I. Title.

PZ7.C85985Mag 2006   [E]
                    QBI06-600132

The Magic Sceptre

The Legend of Blue Santa Claus

Written and Illustrated by

Joan Klatil Creamer

ave you ever wondered how Santa knows what presents to bring or how he visits all the children in the world without being seen? This is a story that has never been told but let's start at the beginning.

In every story and every picture we have always known Santa
in his red suit but there is a Santa who wears not only red
but also blue during the Christmas season.

A few weeks before the holiday, Santa needs to find out what all the
boys and girls want for Christmas. He has to travel the world in a
way that no one will see him.

For this he'll need The Magic Sceptre
with all its wonderful powers.

So Santa gathers Mrs. Claus, the elves, and the reindeer
around the North Pole. Their energy from dancing releases
The Magic Sceptre, which twists and swirls gently into Santa's hands.

Santa then taps The Magic Sceptre three times and says, "Let everyone have the Spirit of Christmas!" and POOF! Santa's suit changes from red to blue and the magic enchantment begins. Now Santa is invisible against the blue of the sky and disappears to human eyes.

At the same time,
the magic sweeps across
Santa's North Pole and changes
his colorful village into a
blue and white wonderland.

Now no one can see the village,
the elves, or Santa's reindeer.

Mrs. Claus, also in her matching blue outfit, loves to bake her special blue sugar cookies with white chocolate chips for Santa and all his helpers.

While munching on the cookies, Santa dreams about new toy ideas.

PRACTICE AREA
FOR
SLIPPERY ROOFTOPS

The reindeer practice and practice to prepare for Christmas Eve.

Santa now begins his work. He travels by his snowy white owl
so the reindeer can rest for their big trip on Christmas Eve.

No one can see Santa as he travels the world, although children have felt the breeze from the owl's giant wings as it magically passes by.

In his blue suit Santa discovers the deepest desires of the children as they write their lists.

The children can't see Santa Claus, of course, but the animals can.

Invisible in blue, like Santa, the elves look for their newly designed toys and watch the children's happy faces.

As Christmas Eve approaches, Santa checks the names and addresses of all the children. The master elf brings Santa the world globe to mark the home of each child.

Even more magic happens on Christmas Eve, when Santa finds
a small chimney or no chimney at all. He just waves The Magic
Sceptre, which makes the sleigh and reindeer small enough to
squeeze through the keyhole.

Upon Santa's arrival,

the littlest members of the family come to see if
Santa has presents for them in his magical bag.

When children awake on Christmas morning, they see their gifts

and know that Santa MUST have been there.

When Santa Claus finally returns to the North Pole,
he once again taps The Magic Sceptre three times and POOF!

Once more Santa is back in his red suit and
the North Pole becomes colorful again.

So as long as you believe in the Spirit of Christmas, "The Magic Sceptre and The Legend of Blue Santa Claus", will live on forevermore.